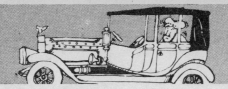

RONNIE AND THE HAUNTED ROLLS ROYCE

When Ronnie discovers a lost, lonely old ghost in the back of his Dad's car, he decides—with the help of his best friend Ethel—to find him a job and a home.

As the ghost is frightened, and rather lazy too, this is not as easy as they expect, but the problem is unexpectedly solved when the car breaks down outside a big old house.

Cover illustration by
Rowan Barnes-Murphy

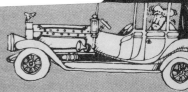

Also by the same author,
and available in Knight Books:

HELP! I AM A PRISONER IN A
TOOTHPASTE FACTORY

THE BOY WITH ILLUMINATED
MEASLES

RONNIE AND THE GREAT
KNITTED ROBBERY

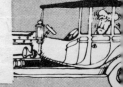

RONNIE AND THE HAUNTED ROLLS ROYCE

JOHN ANTROBUS

Illustrated by
Rowan Barnes-Murphy

KNIGHT BOOKS
Hodder and Stoughton

Copyright © 1982 John Antrobus

First published 1982 by Robson Books Ltd
Knight Books edition 1984
Third impression 1985

British Library C.I.P.

Antrobus, John, *1933–*
 Ronnie and the haunted Rolls Royce.
 I. Title
 823′.914[J]   PZ7

ISBN 0 340 33988 8

Printed and bound in Great Britain for Hodder and
Stoughton Paperbacks, a division of Hodder and
Stoughton Ltd., Mill Road, Dunton Green, Sevenoaks,
Kent (Editorial Office: 47 Bedford Square, London, WC1
3DP) by Cox & Wyman Ltd., Reading

Ronnie and the Haunted Rolls Royce

Ronnie's Dad had a new job. He was a chauffeur. He came home in his new uniform.

"Where's your other clothes?" asked Mum.

"I threw them away," answered Dad, grandly. "From rags to riches in half an hour."

"Where's the car, Dad?" enquired Ronnie, eagerly.

"Oh, I don't get that yet. I have to run in the uniform first. I get a trial week with the uniform and, if I'm managing all right, then they give me a car."

"How did you get the job?" asked Mum, tight-lipped at the change in Dad's appearance. He had gone out in the morning, job hunting, and now he'd come back dressed up to the nines in a new grey uniform, peaked cap, and black leather gloves.

"It's all right, dear, I left my old clothes at work."

'Well, where *is* work?" demanded Mum.

"The Arabian Embassy. I was passing there and I thought I'd go in. I went up to the reception desk. Do

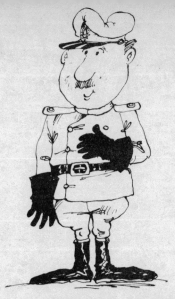

you speak English, I said. No, said the man. What do you want? Well, I said, have you got any good jobs going on your oil rigs?"

"You're not going to Saudi Arabia," Mum said bluntly.

"That's what I told him. Well, he said, we've just bought the top people's store in Knightsbridge, and we're prospecting for oil in the basement."

"I don't fancy that, I told him. No, I don't fancy prospecting for oil in a top people's store in Knightsbridge. Not near Christmas. Have you got anything else? Can you drive a car, he said. Where, I said. Anywhere, he said. I can't go that far, I told him. I have to get home every night. So they fitted me out with this brand new uniform, and they sent me on a trial run with it—through London. When I got back, they examined the uniform for tears and stains. It was immaculate. Full marks, they said. . . ."

Ronnie was laughing. You never knew when Dad was telling the truth. Nor did he, sometimes. Mum looked grim.

"You're the breadwinner in this household," she said.

"That's no laughing matter."

"I know. Let them eat cake." Dad gave Mum a kiss.

"When do you get paid?" she said.

"It's very good money," Dad replied, vaguely. "They showed me some of it. It looked very nice. I'm on commission. I get so much a mile."

"What? Even while you're running in the uniform?" asked Ronnie.

"Oh yes. I was stopped in Bond Street today in this uniform, and a traffic warden came up. What are you doing there? she said. What are you feeding the meter for? You haven't got a car. Don't get funny with me, I said. I can feed the meter if I like. I like meters. Be off with you, you silly woman."

After tea Ronnie went out to play with Ethel. When he told her his Dad had a new job as a chauffeur, she wanted to come back to have a look at the uniform. Dad answered the door in his long, woollen underwear and carpet slippers, though he was still wearing his chauffeur's hat.

"I put the uniform to bed," he said. "It's had a hard day. Ssshh!"

They crept up to the bedroom and had a look at the uniform which was laid out upon the bed. "I'll be sleeping in the spare room tonight," said Dad. "I don't want to disturb it."

"Oh no, you won't," said Mum, breaking the spell as she swept into the room. "Filling these children's heads with nonsense."

"That's what children's heads are for. For filling with nonsense."

Mum picked up the uniform, and they all went down to the kitchen and watched her while she pressed the uniform, filling the room with steam from the iron.

"Coming on foggy," Dad remarked, and his eyes narrowed. "Which reminds me of the time I was fighting the Russians in the Ukraine."

"What happened, Dad?" asked Ronnie.

"I thought I was running away from the front, you see, but when the fog cleared, there I was—standing in the middle of Moscow."

"You weren't even born then," said Mum. "That was your own father fought the Russians in 1920 in the Ukraine."

"It's a family story anyhow," replied Dad. "He handed the story on to me—with his boots."

"Grandad's still alive," interjected Ronnie.

"Now don't you go telling him that. You'll only upset him."

The next evening, to everyone's surprise, Dad came home in a Rolls Royce. He gave a "beep" on the horn as he drove up the street, and curtains were pulled back by inquisitive neighbours. The local children flocked round the rather dilapidated Rolls Royce. Dad proudly climbed out of the car, resplendent in his uniform (though the trousers were a bit short, noticed Ronnie), and old Mrs. Benson hobbled up.

"Oh, that's nice," she said. "You can take me down the 'orspital Thursday."

"Sorry, Mrs. Benson," explained Dad. "This vehicle is not available to take you to hospital. Business only—even I'm not allowed to use it. I have to go to work on the bus and come back for the car later."

"They let you come home in it," she retorted.

"That's because I'm tired. It's the end of a day. I've got good employers. I work for the Sheikhs."

"I got the shakes," she said. "That's why I got to go down the 'orspital." She raised her cane above her head. "How dare you threaten an old age pensioner," she cried.

"I wasn't threatening you, Mrs. Benson."

"Attack is the best form of defence," she shouted. "Charge!" And she started beating the car bonnet with her stick.

Dad intervened. "All right, I'll take you down the hospital. I'm a free taxi service. I'd forgotten that."

Dad went round the front of the car where Charlie Higgins was unscrewing the silver-plated figure. "I'll have that," said Dad, and took off the Rolls mascot, the silver lady known as the "Spirit of Ecstasy".

"Don't you touch my Spirit of Ecstasy," he said, and went indoors.

Ronnie couldn't help feeling a bit disappointed by his Dad's car. He had been expecting a new one.

"Who's 'e drive round in that old banger, then?" asked Charlie.

"Arabs," answered Ronnie.

"How many?"

"A tribe."

"You won't get a tribe in the back of that. You won't get a tribeful in there."

"Oh yes, you will," said Ronnie. "Easy. Often see a tribeful in the back of a Rolls Royce."

"Not with their camels," said the obnoxious boy.

"Do you want a fight?" asked Ronnie, feeling that the family honour was somehow at stake.

Charlie drifted away, however, looking for something more exciting. Ronnie and Ethel remained behind, staring vacantly at the car. Ronnie had particularly wanted to impress her.

"It's haunted," said Ronnie out of the blue, in a desperate effort to make the Rolls sound interesting.

"What?" said Ethel. "Cars ain't haunted."

"This one is. It's got a ghost."

"Well, take it down the garage. They'll get rid of it," suggested Ethel.

"They couldn't," said Ronnie. "Need holy water for that."

"What about that water they put in the batteries?"

"That's distilled water."

"Won't that do?"

"Dunno." Ronnie took a deep breath, and said all in a rush, "If you want to come and sit with me in the car tomorrow night I'll introduce you to the ghost, Ethel."

"All right," said Ethel. "See yer."

She ran home.

The nights were drawing in and it got dark quite early. By the light of a street lamp that filtered into the car, Ronnie and Ethel played ghosts. First Ronnie sat in the front by the wheel and pretended to be a spectral chauffeur taking Her Ladyship to the cemetery where she had to meet a ghoul. Then Ethel climbed over the front and they played racing-drivers in a Grand Prix, with a ghost in the back who had thumbed a lift. Then they both climbed over the back and played a long game of Mothers and Fathers. They were taking their children, twelve in all, to the seaside, and the old Rolls became a boarding-house. It had pull-down tables in the back, and even a little cupboard to make a good dining-room. The dining-room was haunted, so they kept the ghost idea going all evening. But eventually it was time to go home.

"That was good fun," said Ronnie.

"Yeah," agreed Ethel, but she sounded disappointed. "It's not really haunted though, is it?"

"Excuse me," intoned a hollow voice. "I could not help noticing how friendly you were towards ghosts in your games. Excuse me. Oh, ooohhh. Oh, ooohhh—that's a few groans and sighs to identify myself—Aah me! The Count! He bricked me in. Ooohhh!"

"Bricked you in to a Rolls Royce?" asked Ronnie.

"No, no, no. I was bricked up behind a wall of the old stables of a manor house. I was a simple young gardener at the time. Excuse me. Oh dearie me! That makes me feel a lot better. A good old dearie me, and a good groan. Yes, where was I?"

"At the manor house," said Ronnie, enjoying the conversation with a disembodied voice. Ethel did not look very scared either.

"Oh yes," said the ghost. "By the way, do you want the rattling of chains? Or the grinding of gear boxes in this case?"

"Just tell us your story," Ronnie prompted.

"Yes. Ohhh. Ooohhh. Well, the wicked Count was raging *avec* jealousy—as we would say in those days—a *crime passionnel* was on the cards because the Countess was most beautiful and the Count was a most unattractive fellow. Follow so far?"

"Go on," said Ronnie and Ethel in unison.

"I had a fresh, open-air bloom then, and the Count became morbidly obsessed that his wife was growing much too friendly with me. He came upon us in the rose garden one day, you know."

"What were you doing?" asked Ethel.

"Pruning the roses. So he—Oh dear! Oh dearie me! He bricked me up inside the stables. Made a very good job of it. He liked building walls. Bricklaying was his hobby. Nothing he liked better than to brick up a servant . . ."

"Hurry. I've got to go home," said Ethel. "My Mum said I'd got to be in by eight, or else!"

"How did you get in the Rolls Royce?" insisted Ronnie.

"I'm coming to that. Years later the wall was demolished, when the stables were made into garages, and this Rolls Royce was parked in there."

"Did it belong to the Count?" enquired Ethel.

"No. This was over three hundred years later. That

Count wasn't very well by then. In fact he was dead."

"Get on with it," Ronnie pleaded. "We'll get into trouble if we don't go in. Can't you show yourself to us?"

"No. Not on my ectoplasm allowance. I have only enough to show myself once every seventy years. I'm not going to waste it on a couple of Herberts like you."

"Right," said Ethel, determinedly. "I'm off. Our games were more interesting than the real ghost."

"Oh dear! Bricked up behind a wall because of a soppy Countess. I decided to haunt the Rolls Royce one day," the ghost gabbled, "and I must have fallen asleep. I woke up on the M1. Next thing I knew I'd been sold; I tried to adjust, but I kept getting sold and I ended up with a bunch of Arabs. Well—the car was sold, and that came to the same thing. I can't go home now—I hardly know where I am."

"We'll think of something," said Ronnie. "Goodnight."

The children went home. Ronnie didn't tell his Mum and Dad about the ghost. They would put it down to his lively imagination. Before Ronnie went to sleep that night he decided he would help the ghost to do what it wanted to do—if he could find out what it was.

On Thursday morning Dad took Mrs. Benson to the hospital on his way to work.

"I'll use the car this morning," he told her.

"Save yer coming back for it," said Mrs. Benson.

She had to make another appointment for the following Saturday morning. This time Ronnie and Ethel managed to persuade Dad to take them along for the ride, for by now Mrs. Benson was used to her personal taxi service.

"Get your buttons polished up," she said to Dad.

"I'll want you in uniform."

"They're made of plastic, Mrs. Benson," Dad told her good-naturedly.

"And either let your trousers down or pull your socks up. Remember I'm in the back! It all reflects on me, your appearance."

"Yes, Mrs. Benson."

As soon as Dad and Mrs. Benson were in the hospital Ronnie asked, "Are you there, ghost?"

"No," replied the ghost. "No voices or visitations before ten o'clock."

"Let's tell Mrs. Benson," suggested Ethel. "She might believe us."

"All right," agreed Ronnie.

On the way back from the hospital Dad had to stop for a pound of haddock. "Won't be long," he said, as he parked near the fishmonger and joined the queue.

"Mrs. Benson," said Ronnie. "This car is haunted."

"I thought I detected a presence," she replied. "I knew it was either something from the spirit world, or cats had been in here."

"Ooohhh dearie me! Aah me!" said the ghost.

"Are you there?" asked Mrs. Benson.

"Well, where do you think I am?" demanded the ghost.

"O spirit!" intoned Mrs. Benson, while the children kept watch for Dad's return. "Go and fetch Mr. Benson —and ask him where he hid the silver fish knives and forks."

"I'm not a messenger," grumbled the ghost. "I'm of this world."

"You're a spirit, ain't yer?" demanded Mrs. Benson.

"But I am trapped in this world. If I was able to go to the spirit world, I wouldn't be here."

"Fetch Mr. Benson," she commanded.

"You fetch Mr. Benson," sulked the ghost.

"I shall free you to go to the spirit world," said Mrs. Benson.

"Well, if you can do that I'll send Mr. Benson back with the knives and forks."

"He can't have taken 'em with him! But I'll bet he knows where they are."

Dad came back with the fish, and the spirited conversation stopped.

"Can I sit in the car tonight again? With Ethel?" asked Ronnie, when they got home.

"All right," said Dad. "Just the two of you now."

"And Mrs. Benson, please?" pleaded Ronnie.

"I'll be there," said Mrs. Benson, as Dad helped her out of the car, "don't worry." She turned to Dad. "Take the rest of the day off," she said.

That night, Ronnie, Ethel, and Mrs. Benson sat in the back of the car. Dad looked out of the window at them.

"They're having a lovely time."

"With the nonsense that you put into their heads, I'm not surprised," retorted Mum. "That Mrs. Benson's as bad. You'll have the whole neighbourhood sitting in there soon."

"It's very popular," agreed Dad.

"Come and play Space Invaders," said Mum, and Dad reluctantly left the window.

"Are you there, O spirit?" asked Mrs. Benson, tapping her stick three times on the floor. The children, who were in the front of the car, leaned over the back, watching with great interest.

"Yes, I am here Mrs. Benson," replied the ghost.

"Materialize!" ordered Mrs. Benson.

"I am not wasting seventy years' ectoplasm on you!"

said the ghost.

"You won't need it in the spirit world to which I shall release you."

"Seeing's believing," said the ghost.

"All join hands," she instructed, "and say after me:

Hey diddle diddle,
The cat and the fiddle,
The Count is forgiven,
And the pig's in the middle."

They all repeated the verse, but the ghost hadn't quite heard what she'd said. "The pig's in the what?" he asked.

"You are now released!" cried Mrs. Benson.

"Am I?" said the ghost.

"Fetch Mr. Benson, and return with him this time tomorrow night."

"You make it all sound very easy," whined the ghost.

"You needed a good woman to tell you what to do, hanging around on earth. Everyone needs to be told. No good hanging around with your hands in your pockets. Begone!" she suddenly shouted. There was a whooshing sound, then silence. "He's gone," she said. "Same time tomorrow night."

The next evening Ronnie went up to his Dad. "Dad," he said, "I've arranged for Mrs. Benson and Ethel to sit with me in the car again tonight. You don't mind?"

"You'll be wearing out the upholstery." Dad gave Ronnie the car key. "Tonight's the last night you can have it."

That night they sat in the car, Ronnie, Ethel and Mrs. Benson. She tapped three times with her stick. It was dark inside the car because tonight the nearby street lamp wasn't even flickering. It wasn't working at all.

"I'm really frightened this time," said Ethel.

"I'll hold your hand," said Ronnie. He took her hand, and they both felt better.

"Materialize!" commanded Mrs. Benson.

An unearthly glow pervaded the Rolls Royce and there—in the driver's seat—appeared the ghost of the gardener.

"Ooohhh," he said. "Ooohhh—is that enough? I'm never sure. Aah me! Seventy years' ectoplasm gone for a Burton—how do I look?"

"Dreadful," said Ethel.

"Well, dreadful's better than nothing," replied the ghost. "Oh, when I think what a fresh, young bloom I had once . . ."

"Is that why the Countess fancied you? Because you were rosy?"

"Well, she was a bit of a blossom herself. I haven't got time to go into all that."

"Did you get Mr. Benson?" demanded Mrs. Benson.

"Only his voice. He was too scared to come in person in case you whacked him with your stick, like you did when he was alive."

"He never complained. I thought he didn't mind," pondered Mrs. Benson. "Are you there, Mr. Benson?" she suddenly shouted.

"Yes. What you want, Matilda?"

"What did you do with the silver fish knives and forks, you old fool?"

"I sold 'em and spent the money down the Prince of Wales, making myself popular in the saloon bar."

Mrs. Benson raised her stick. "Popular! You ain't popular now! Where are you, you rogue? I'll bash the living daylights out of your ectoplasms." She thrashed round the interior of the car with her stick.

"He's gone! He's gone! Careful!" exclaimed the ghost.

"I'll go after him!" she declared.

"He's got a few years' start on you," chuckled the ghost. "I am released now. Thank you, Mrs. Benson, for that good spell. Aah me! Bye bye. Oh dearie me! Thank you, children, for being friendly. Farewell." The voice was growing fainter, and the last they heard was a weak "Oh dearie meee"—or it might have been the sound the old leather upholstery made as Mrs. Benson slid across to open the door.

"Come on, young Ethel," she said. "It's after eight o'clock. I'd better take you home, or your mum'll give you what for."

"What for?" asked Ethel.

"I don't know," said Mrs. Benson. "Let's go and ask her."

Ronnie Meets Count
de String

Ronnie knew that the ghost from the Rolls Royce had been exorcised and expelled by old Mrs. Benson to go freely into the spirit world—but did that mean it would not come back?

While Ronnie was playing with Ethel one morning they both got a bit fed up and hot and tired, and they sat back wondering what they could do to renew their interest in life.

"Do you think that ghost would come back if we asked it?" said Ronnie.

"Where from?" said Ethel.

"Well, wherever they go. I mean, what's a ghost supposed to do if it's not haunting."

"Nothing," said Ethel. "No, a ghost ain't doing nothing if it's not haunting."

"You mean it's unemployed? In that case it would have to go down the Labour Exchange."

"And sign on as an unemployed ghost?"

"Yes, till a haunting job came up again."

That night they borrowed the keys to the car and sat in the back of the Rolls Royce again. They had decided to call the ghost back to the material world. Ethel couldn't bear to think of it having to sign on.

"Come back!" commanded Ronnie. "Come back, ghost, wherever you are."

"Oh, dearie me," said the ghost, and a fluorescent light shimmered in the back of the car. "What do you want now?"

Ethel said, "You should be haunting."

"Oh no I shouldn't," said the ghost. "I am resting in another sphere."

"Look," said Ronnie, "you remember you were

bricked up behind a wall by the wicked Count some centuries ago?"

"Oh yes."

"Well, what did you do then?"

"I put a curse on the whole family. For ever and ever. Aah me!" The light seemed to shiver and Ethel shivered too.

"Oh, dear," she said.

"Oh, dearie *me*," said the ghost. "Then I forgot all about it. Let bygones be bygones, I said to myself."

"But ghosts can't do that," insisted Ronnie. "If you put a curse on the family for all generations you've got to keep it going."

"It's awfully hard work, you know," complained the ghost.

"Well, you shouldn't have put it on for ever and ever. You'll have to go back to do your haunting. That's why you are a ghost. We'll have to find out where that family lives, and then we can take you back there, and you can continue cursing for all eternity."

"Eternity's much too long," moaned the ghost. "How about every Thursday afternoon? Anyway, I don't know where they live now. They've probably moved—it's been a long time."

"What were the people called?" asked Ethel.

The ghost didn't answer, and was silent for so long they wondered if he'd gone.

"Ghost? Are you there? We'll never talk to you again if you don't tell us."

"I can't remember." The ghost sounded sulky.

"All right," said Ronnie. "We'll find out who they are, and deliver you back to them."

The next day Ronnie had a brainwave. He looked in all the compartments of the Rolls Royce; in one, in the dashboard, was the old log book. This listed all the people who had ever owned the car, and was much more interesting than the boring Vehicle Registration Document from Swansea.

The car seemed to have had half a dozen previous owners, but the very first one was given as Count Jeffry de Strong. That must be it, thought Ronnie. That must be the cursed family!

The Count's address was Strainedway House (open to the Public every Tuesday and Thursday), and Ronnie planned to persuade Dad to take them there for an outing. It could be an Easter holiday treat.

Dad got time off, and took a carload to Strainedway House. He didn't know how much of a treat the children had planned it to be—taking the ghost.

Mum, and Ethel's Mum, and Mrs. Benson came along too. "I haven't got anything better to do," she told them.

In the Baronial Hall Dad said, "I'm going for a programme or catalogue or something. Wait here." Mum wasn't listening to him. She and Ethel's mum and Mrs. Benson had seen a room full of old furniture, and they were off.

"I could do with a good sit-down," Mrs. Benson was saying. "Those Chippendale chairs look comfortable."

Ronnie and Ethel were left alone.

"Did you want a catalogue?"

They turned to face a thin, gaunt man who wore a piece of string round his neck, where most men would have had a tie.

"Dad's gone to get one," explained Ronnie.

"Most unfortunate," said the man. "They were here all the time. In the hallway, where you'd expect to find them.

"Are you Count de Strong?" asked Ethel.

"No," said the man, "though I was born Jeffry de

Strong. But when the family fortunes failed I had to sort parcels for the Post Office, and I was always bringing string home—little bits of string which you might find lying around. Indeed, I now have a world-famous collection of string. When my father passed on I became the Count, but my name is now Jeffry de String. It seems more fitting."

"You are cursed," said Ethel.

"Yes," agreed the Count. "That is so. It's a wretched habit, really, collecting—ah! There's a piece!"

He darted off to one side, and swooped on a piece of string that lay on the floor.

"This must be labelled and dated—time and place—and added to my collection," he said with satisfaction, but misery showed in his eyes.

"Your curse is worse than collecting string," said Ronnie knowingly.

"Ohh." The Count's eyes narrowed. "What do you know about me? Do you know about the magic properties of string? Do you know that they who never cut string cannot slip into a time warp? It's a fact. Little known. I never cut string. And why? Because I don't want to fall into a hole in time. I've got string of all lengths, for any emergencies!" He was shouting now. "Got any parcels you want tied up, have you?"

"No," said Ronnie.

"Pity."

"Your curse lies deeper than that," said Ronnie.

"What? What, you mean it's worse than string? What have you come to tell me?" he asked as he led them down a dark corridor and into his study, shutting the door behind them. The room was full of display cases in which were many little balls of string, all neatly done up and labelled.

"You are honoured," said the Count. "Feast your eyes. For instance, this wonderful little ball here." He picked up a white piece of string with a red fleck in it. "I found this in Trafalgar Square on Christmas Eve, 1975."

Ronnie said, "String is meaningless, except for doing things up."

"That's right," Ethel backed him up.

"Oh, yes?" sneered the Count.

"Look," said Ronnie. "I'll prove to you that your anxiety has got nothing to do with string." Ronnie took out his penknife and cut the piece of string. The Count shrank back in horror. His string, carefully collected throughout his lifetime, really did have magical properties. The room spun round, and they entered a hole in time.

Ronnie and Ethel found themselves in a rose garden. There was no sign of the Count de String, but the big house nearby was certainly Strainedway House—it looked newly built. A gardener appeared and began to prune the roses.

"That's the ghost," whispered Ronnie.

"He doesn't look like a ghost now," said Ethel.

"Yes, but perhaps we do," said Ronnie, as the gardener walked right through them.

"He can't see us," said Ethel. "He just walked right through us."

"Yes," said Ronnie. "Obviously something has happened to us."

"Course it has," said Ethel. "I'm not used to people walking through me. You shouldn't have cut that string, should you? He warned us."

"I didn't know it was magic string, Ethel," Ronnie replied. "I thought it was just for doing up parcels. I didn't know if you cut it with a penknife you'd fall into a hole in time."

"Now look what you've done," cried Ethel. "It's Brownies tonight. How am I going to get back in time?"

"Leave it to me," said Ronnie confidently.

"I did that before," she said. "That's how we got here."

A lady who looked like the Countess (for she was wearing a costume of three centuries ago) came into the rose garden. She sighed mightily, and took the gardener by the hand.

"Sweet William," she said. "Tonight we must elope together."

"But I've got to look after the garden, madam," said the gardener.

"Nonsense. Let it run to seed," replied the Countess, and she fell into his arms.

"You can't let roses run to seed, madam," stated the simple gardener. "Constant pruning improves blooming."

Just then the Count walked round the corner. The children noted that he too was wearing very old-fashioned clothes.

"We've definitely fallen through a hole in time," whispered Ronnie.

"Right!" snapped the Count. "Trifle with her ladyship, would you? You shall be bricked up into the stable wall for your impertinence!"

The Count looked remarkably like Jeffry de String, but must have been an earlier Count—de Strong. He dragged the gardener to the stable wall, and then began to brick him in.

"I love a bit of bricklaying," said the Count and whistled as he worked.

"I know that tune," said the gardener, and joined in.

"You will be bricked up in this wall forever!" warned

the Count. "How dare you plan to elope with her Ladyship!"

"I only planned to prune the roses, sir," answered the simple-hearted gardener, "when her Ladyship came and swooned in my arms." He was taking a great interest in the wall building, and even helped from the other side by setting the bricks straight.

"Where will you be putting the door, sir?" he enquired.

"Door? There won't be a door. You will be bricked in for ever. For all eternity! You won't need a door."

"I see, sir. Yes, sir. As you say, sir," answered the artless gardening man. "We'll just have a little window then—so I can see out and wave at people."

"No waving," said the Count firmly. "Certainly not. Of course you can't have a window."

"Well, how are people going to pass food in then?" puzzled the gardener.

"You won't be getting any food." The last brick was waiting to be placed.

"No food, sir?" The gardener peered through the slit. "I shall get very hungry. No food? For ever? That's a long time, sir, begging your pardon."

"Well, you'll have to haunt me," said the Count de Strong. "Bring down a curse upon me, man, and upon all the generations to come. Come on, do your worst."

"Well, if you insist, sir."

"I do. Every reputable family has a ghost. You must be good for something. Haunt our family, and our household for ever unto the last Jeffry, do you hear me?"

"How many of them will there be, sir?"

"Well, every Jeffry has a Jeffry, then that Jeffry has a Jeffry, and so on. The main thing is to keep the family line going down through the ages."

"And I've got to curse all of them?"

"Certainly!"

"Very well, sir," said the obedient servant, the loyal pruner of the Count's roses. "Will that be all, sir? Do have the roses cut back by the third of October every year, sir."

"Farewell," said the Count cheerfully. "Is there anything else?" and he shoved in the last brick, catching his fingers. "Curses!" he yelled.

"Yes, I won't forget the curses, sir," came a muffled voice from inside the wall.

The children couldn't help laughing. The Count turned to her Ladyship.

"Was that you tittering, dear?"

"No, Jeffry," she replied.

They went off, arm in arm, towards Strainedway House.

"So that's how it happened," said Ronnie.

"Can't we go now?" said Ethel. "I don't want to be late for Brownies."

The Count turned back a moment and shouted at the wall. "Are you there, Curse of the Jeffries?"

"Yes, sir. Still here, sir."

"When you haunt the Baronial Hall don't use the suit of armour—it creaks too much, and will keep everyone awake."

"Right, sir. Anything else, sir?" came the faint voice of the faithful retainer.

"Groaning's all right in moderation, and remember to say 'Aah me, aah me'."

"I was never in the army, sir."

The gardener's voice faded away, and the Count, looking rather pensive, rejoined his wife. "I have given him all his instructions for eternity," confirmed the Count. "I think he'll make an excellent family ghost."

When they were alone again, Ethel said, "You don't know how to get us back to our own time, do you?"

"Yes, I do," said Ronnie, and whistled.

"Whistling won't do it," said Ethel.

"It helps," replied Ronnie. He spotted two bits of string lying on the lawn. It was the very same string that he had cut in two. On impulse he picked up the pieces and tied them together.

Instantly they were back in the study with the Count Jeffry de String of their own time.

The Count said, "I saw it all. It was as if I were my ancestor in that scene. So that is the true curse of the de Strings—or the de Strongs, as we then were. We bricked up a gardener and he has to haunt us for ever. Well, where is he?"

"Out in the Rolls Royce," said Ronnie.

They went out into the car park and all climbed in the back of Dad's Rolls Royce.

"Appear, ghost," commanded Ronnie.

Nothing happened.

"Stop mucking about," said Ethel. "Come on, ghost, we know you're there."

"Oh, dearie me. Aah me!" A thin vaporous cloud formed, and the cringing shape of the gardener could be made out.

"So that's you!" cried out Jeffry de String. "You rascal! You rogue! You scallywag! Where have you been all these years when you should have been haunting us?"

"Oh dearie me. It's a sorry story, sir. After I was bricked up three centuries ago in your stable wall I knew it was my duty to haunt you, but I was too shy."

"Too shy, man?" cried Count Jeffry de String—last in a long line of Strong, Strong, Strong and Strong String.

"Well," the ghost coughed apologetically. "I didn't know if I'd be welcome up at the big house, sir. It was a step up the social ladder for me. I'd never set foot in there before—me a simple gardener, a rose pruner."

"You fool!"

"And a fool, sir, yes."

"You had been promoted to be the curse of the Jeffries. It was your duty to haunt the big house, not skulk around haunting the brick wall. What good's that? No one would notice that! And what were you doing in the Rolls? Don't I recognize this machine?"

"Yes, sir. It was your father's originally, sir, before the family fell on hard times and you had to work at the PO."

"The PO?"

"The Post Office, sir," explained the ghost. "Aah me! Your father, the last spendthrift Jeffry, pulled down the wall, sir, to make a garage. So I got in the Rolls when he put it in there."

"That was damned impertient of you. We didn't want our Rolls Royce haunted."

"That's why I kept quiet, sir. And when you sold it, sir, I went with it. I've had a succession of owners."

"Come back with me into Strainedway House immediately," commanded the Count. "You must take up your haunting duties. You have no need to be shy."

"I'll see you by the wainscot tonight then, sir," said the obedient ghost, and disappeared.

"Thank you," said Count Jeffry to the children. "Do come round some Saturday afternoon and take the ghost out. Haunting should be very good for business. Tourists, you know. Refound the family fortunes. But I must let the poor chap have some time off. Ta-ta."

He climbed out of the car, and paused. "I shall be able to give up my world-famous collection of string now," he said. "Yes, being haunted is much more interesting. String was a poor substitute for the real thing, the true curse of the Jeffries." And he strode away happily into Strainedway House.

Dad came out a little later with Mum. Mrs. Benson was talking to Ethel's mum. "That's the last time I'll sit down in a Chippendale," she was saying. "They look better than they feel. That's why they discontinued them, I expect."

"Funny," Dad said as they all got into the car. "I was by the wainscoting in the library when I felt a presence. It sent my hair standing on end, what's left of it. I suppose it was nothing, but some of these old houses *are* haunted."

He drove them home, and Mum got a big tea ready with lots of hot buttered scones.

"You look a bit pale, dear," she remarked to Dad. "Seen a ghost, have you?"

"You know, I might well have done," replied Dad thoughtfully.

"Now don't you go putting ideas into the children's heads," Mum warned him. Ronnie and Ethel kept quiet. They didn't *need* any ideas putting into their heads—not about ghosts, anyway.

The Ghost Seeks New Employment

There was a rattle on the window pane. Ronnie woke up. It was the middle of the night.

"Oh, dearie me. Aah me," he heard a voice sigh.

"If it's you, ghost, why are you outside the window when you could just as easily materialize inside the room?" whispered Ronnie, then louder, "Can you hear me?"

"Oh yes, don't shout. You're frightening me. I *am*

inside the room. I rattled on the window to wake you up."

"What do you want?" demanded Ronnie.

"It's Count Jeffry de String. He's ill-treating me, demanding that I haunt the mansion day and night. He has coachloads of American tourists in. He's determined to refound the family fortunes."

"Why can't you refuse to appear?" asked Ronnie. He peered into the shadows of his moonlit room, but he could only hear the voice, not see the shape.

"It's no good looking for me," exclaimed the ghost. "I'm right out of ectoplasm. I've been borrowing some from other ghosts—I'm in a lot of debt."

"What do you want me to do about it?" said Ronnie, not unkindly.

"Hide me. When he calls I have to come. He invokes my name. Come, he calls, the Curse of the Jeffries—and I have to answer."

"Look," said Ronnie, "he can't hurt you if you refuse to appear."

"Oh, he can," the ghost cried, and chains rattled. "He can. Aah me! First of all he can set the cat on me. Ghosts don't like cats. He puts the cat out at night when I do most of my haunting."

"But if you don't appear the cat can't get you either."

"Oh dearie me," cried the ghost. "I have a contract to appear—twice nightly. He made me sign it."

"You let people dominate you too easily," scolded Ronnie. "What did you get in return?"

"Well, I'm mentioned in the catalogue as the Curse of the Jeffries—and there's talk of a book . . ."

"It's vanity," said Ronnie. "You want to be well known."

"Yes, I do want to be famous," admitted the ghost reluctantly.

"That takes a lot of work," Ronnie told him. "You

can't just haunt when you feel like it then run away 'cos you're frightened of the cat."

"I need a holiday," complained the ghost.

"We're going to the seaside tomorrow," announced Ronnie.

"Oh," said the ghost, and disappeared.

Ronnie and his Mum and Dad and Ethel and her parents were all going to the seaside on holiday together. They'd invited Mrs. Benson, but she said she could *see* quite enough at home, thank you.

"Send me a postcard," she'd asked, and Mum had got quite cross with Dad when he wanted to buy one of a very fat lady in a swimsuit. They sent her one of the pier instead.

"It looks quite like her," said Dad, but Ronnie was listening to Ethel.

"Let's go and be ill on the roundabouts," she suggested.

"I don't want to be ill," answered Ronnie.

"Don't you want to be sick?"

"Not much."

"You're not much fun," pouted Ethel. "I'm always sick after I've been on the roundabouts. What's the good of coming to the seaside if you're not going to be sick?"

"I don't like being sick," countered Ronnie.

"Nor do I," admitted Ethel. "But it's nice afterwards."

Eventually, Ethel persuaded Ronnie to spend some of their precious money and time on the roundabouts in the fairground. They got on to a particularly vicious-looking affair that not only went round but in and out in a zigzag. As soon as it started up Ethel yelled out, "I want to get off! I want to get off! Tell the man to stop it!"

Ronnie laughed. Soon the ride was over and Ethel wasn't sick, but she did look decidedly green.

"Why did you want to get off?" asked Ronnie. "I mean why did you want to get on when all you wanted to do was get off?"

"You can't get off until you've got on—don't be daft!" And that was all Ronnie could get out of her on the subject.

They came up to the ghost train ride. Ronnie wanted to go on this one. Ethel was reluctant.

"Come on," said Ronnie. "You know we like ghosts. Our ghost from the Rolls came on holiday with us."

"Where is he?" asked Ethel.

"I don't know. I heard him in the Rolls saying, 'Oh dearie, dearie me' on the way here. He's hiding from Count Jeffry de String," and he told Ethel about the busloads of American tourists.

"Still," she said, "it can't be very difficult to hide if you're a ghost and invisible most of the time."

They boarded the ghost train. Phantoms and skeletons beset them on the jerky ride. Daggers loomed and red blood seemed to drip from the ceiling. It was very good. Suddenly the train stopped in mid-tunnel, and a voice said, "Oh, dearie me. Aah me!"

"What are you doing here, ghost?" whispered Ronnie.

"I'm working," answered the ghost. "The owner of the ghost train ride has promised me fame and glory—and I don't have to work in the winters."

"That's much better than working for the dreadful Count," said Ethel.

"Yes," said the ghost. "And there aren't any cats here. It's much better."

"Why did you stop the train?" asked Ronnie.

"I've been able to put a gremlin in the works," explained the ghost. "Would you like to meet him?"

"Yes, please," the children exclaimed simultaneously.

A gremlin appeared, only a little man to be sure, in a green beret.

"Hello," he said. "I'm a gremlin. I get into the works. If you have an electric mixer at home and it stops––it's probably a gremlin. Or a lawn-mower that breaks down for no reason at all, or an electric toothbrush that won't work—it's an even bet it's one of my little friends. And why? Because we like to be busy all day long, all the time, interfering with working machines!"

The gremlin started singing.

> "*If something goes wrong*
> *Like an end to a song*
> *If you find it won't rhyme*
> *Keep strict dancing time*
> *It's probably a gremlin.*
> *If the mixer won't work*
> *Won't iron that shirt . . .*
> *Kettle's on the blink*
> *While Dad's shaving in the sink*
> *Mum's iron rings a lot . . .*
> *While the telephone gets hot*
> *It's probably a gremlin.*"

"That's an awful song," interrupted Ronnie, laughing.

"That's hardly a song at all," scolded Ethel.

"Good! Good!" The gremlin danced up and down. "It was a rotten song! That's 'cos it was a gremlin song!"

The man who ran the ghost train ride came along the tunnel with a spanner, and the gremlin immediately disappeared.

"Oh dearie me," sighed the ghost. "What fun! What a companion!" He sounded nearly happy. The man adjusted a few bolts, and left the tunnel. Ronnie and Ethel were the only ones in that bend of the tunnel, and nobody else had seen the gremlin.

"That's a very bad influence on the ghost," declared Ethel. "Here we are teaching him to haunt properly and do a good day's work—which every ghost should do—and then he runs away from home and gets a job at the seaside, he doesn't tell anyone where he's going and then he takes up with a gremlin."

"Yes," agreed Ronnie, "but isn't he funny?" He had liked the gremlin, and his silly song.

"Just causing mischief," said Ethel. "That ain't responsible, is it?"

The train started up and soon they were out in the daylight again. They found Mum asleep in a deck chair, while Dad was inventing a device to keep the sand out of sandwiches. Ethel's mum and dad were having a nice paddle. So many good treats followed on the sands in the next few days—riding donkeys, sea bathing, building sandcastles (none of which survived the tide), that all concern for the ghost and his companion left them. That is, until they were on their way home.

On the way home the Rolls Royce broke down. Ronnie and Ethel were in the back, as Mum had elected to travel with Ethel's parents, and let the children travel together. Mum had left earlier so that there would be tea when they got home.

"Oh dear," said Dad, his head buried under the bonnet. "It's a gremlin to be sure."

His face covered in oil, Dad set off down the road, looking for a garage. Immediately the gremlin appeared, singing,

> "*I'm a little gremlin*
> *I sing a happy song.*
> *I'm always doing mischief*
> *And making things go wrong.*
> *I'm always doing naughty things*
> *So nothing can go right,*
> *Everything is breaking down*
> *Around me day and night.*"

"Mmmm," he frowned. "That song was a very good one. That's the only thing that was wrong with it. I must try harder to make it a bad song. It's not easy, you know. Things have a tendency to work if left on their own. It's only the gremlins that make chaos possible."

"You should be ashamed of yourself," Ethel told him.

"Why? I never rest when there's mischief to be done. Haha!"

"Oh dearie me," chimed in the ghost. "What good company! We had to leave the ghost train because the man running it sold up. His trains kept breaking down."

"That's because of me," boasted the gremlin.

"Where are you going now?" asked Ronnie.

"To do more mischief," declared the gremlin. "Wherever that takes us. There's always mischief to be done. There's always some machine that needs a helping hand to bring it grinding to a halt."

Dad came back with a garage mechanic, and the voices stopped.

Dad said, "When I try to start her up, nothing happens."

To demonstrate this he turned on the ignition, and the engine purred into life.

"That's funny," said Dad.

"That'll be five pounds," said the mechanic.

"Five pounds! You haven't done anything yet!" Dad exploded.

"No. Doing things is extra," said the man.

"Not for me it's not," said Dad, and he jumped in the car and drove off.

Later, as the sun was setting—they were already late because of the delay—the car stopped again.

"Oh dear," said Dad. "It's a gremlin, you can bet on it."

But nothing Dad could do would get the car started again.

"I'll have to fetch help," said Dad. "I'm going to phone the RAC. You two stay here."

Dad disappeared into the dusk.

The gremlin hopped up and down on the bonnet. "That fooled him."

"You're not so clever," said Ronnie. "He said it was a gremlin, my Dad."

"They sometimes say it, but they never believe it. They never act on it."

"What is the best way to deal with gremlins?" asked Ethel craftily.

"Lose interest in them. They like to be appreciated. A gremlin in the works can only stop the works while he stays in the works. So if you wait a little while, he goes away to find something else to do."

"Why are you keeping company with the ghost?" asked Ronnie.

"To help him become rich and famous," said the gremlin. "We've teamed up."

"Teamed up, that's it," agreed the ghost. "Aah me! What good fun we have!" He was quiet for a while, just chuckling now and then as he thought over his adventures with the gremlin.

It was growing late, and still Dad did not return.

"Let's go up to that big house over there," said Ronnie, pointing out a house that was silhouetted against the sky.

"Oh dearie me," said the ghost. "Don't go up there. It might be haunted."

But go up there they did. The ghost went with them, for he was too frightened to stay on his own. The gremlin didn't go. The only thing that would attract him was another piece of working machinery into which he could insert himself with his tricks.

They found a door and pulled on the bell; it jangled somewhere inside the old house, which looked vaguely familiar to Ronnie.

"It must be deserted," whispered Ethel.

"Wait a minute. Someone's coming," answered Ronnie.

The door creaked open and a cobwebbed butler stood before them. When he spoke it seemed that dust flew from his mouth, so long had it been since he had had a conversation.

"What . . . do . . . you . . . want?" he enquired.

"Did my Dad call here to make a phone call?" asked Ronnie.

"No."

Ronnie noticed Dad's cap was lying on a table just inside the door.

"All right," he said.

The butler shut the door.

"Dad's in there," said Ronnie. "This is where he must have come to phone the RAC."

An owl hooted.

The ghost spoke up. "I'll go and have a look. Oh dearie me. Aah me!"

He shimmered before them for a second then vanished through the door into the house. The children waited. Suddenly there were yells and screams. The door flew open and the butler and three other men ran down the drive. The ghost, chains rattling, floated through the air and followed them.

"Oh, dearie me," he said as he passed Ronnie and Ethel. "There's no such thing as coincidence. Do you know where we are? This is the back entrance to Strainedway House. I'd forgotten the Count was going to be away for a week. Excuse me—I must go and frighten the burglars a bit more. Fancy one of them dressing up as a butler! Bye for now."

"He sounded nearly brave," said Ronnie. "Let's go in and see where Dad is."

Ronnie's Dad was in what looked like the Count's study, tied up. He started to tell them all about it even before they'd finished getting the ropes off.

"Robbers," he said. "Stripping the house down, they were. Old fireplaces worth a fortune, stained-glass windows, wood panelling, Chippendale chairs . . ." He waved an arm, shaking off the last bit of rope, and stood up. He went over to the Count's telephone and rang first the police, then the RAC.

"That's that, then," he said. "We'll go back to the car to wait for the RAC." Ethel and Ronnie followed him out of the house, and sat quietly in the back seat while they waited for the RAC van to turn up. The ghost had rejoined them, but they weren't going to tell Dad that.

At last the RAC mechanic arrived, and when he tried the starter, the car engine purred into life immediately.

"It must be a gremlin," said Dad.

"No charge," said the RAC man. "There's quite a few gremlins around these parts. The police have just caught a vanload of thieves up the road—their engine was stalling and starting all over the place. One of them had dressed up as an ancient retainer. They'd been trying to burgle the Count de String's house up there." He pointed at Strainedways House and Dad nodded wisely.

The gremlin appeared at the left-hand back window, where Dad wouldn't see who Ronnie and Ethel were talking to. "That was fun," he said. "Bye bye."

"Aren't you coming with us?"

"No. I can't resist an engine that's beautifully tuned up." The gremlin disappeared towards the RAC van.

Dad got into the Rolls Royce, started the car and drove home to a very late tea and a worried Mum. The RAC man had no such luck. He had to arrange a tow home—he had a gremlin in the works. The towing lorry

arrived all right, but then that couldn't start. There were an awful lot of gremlins, or one awful gremlin doing a lot of work.

The next morning Count Jeffry de String arrived at Ronnie's house and knocked on the door. The bell wasn't working—but it probably wasn't a gremlin. Dad had been trying to invent a bell that would ask who a visitor was.

Count Jeffry thanked everyone for their help in catching the robbers, and then added a strange request. He wanted Dad to take him to meet his employers, the Arab sheikhs.

At the embassy the Count did a deal with the sheikh, and bought back the Rolls, paying rather more than it was worth. Dad arrived home that night with the story.

"I'm out of a job again. They've given me the uniform, though."

"And a golden handshake?" asked Mum.

"No. The only shake I got was an oil sheikh giving me two weeks' money in lieu of notice."

"Count Jeffry's got the Rolls for keeps, then?" asked Ronnie.

"That's right," said Dad. "He told me his father was the first owner. There's a coincidence."

Later, when Ronnie told Ethel all about it, they decided that Count Jeffry had been more keen to get back his ghost—whose favourite haunt was the Rolls Royce—than to resume ownership of the car.

"Perhaps he'll let him stay in the car now," said Ronnie, "and maybe even take him on little trips. It's no good working ghosts too hard, you know—they run away."

"Yes," said Ethel, "they do. I hope the Count remembers to keep the car windows closed at night."

"Why?" puzzled Ronnie.

"So's the cat can't get in."

THE BOY WITH ILLUMINATED MEASLES

JOHN ANTROBUS

One morning when Ronnie looked in the mirror he saw that he was covered in spots – red ones, yellow ones, green and blue – and they flashed on and off like lights on a Christmas tree!

The spots take Ronnie on a breathtaking chase round the world, pursued by those who want to discover the secret of his illuminated measles.

The first in a series of hilarious adventures with fast-paced plots and an eccentric hero.

A Royal Mail service in association with the Book Marketing Council & The Booksellers Association.

Post-A-Book is a Post Office trademark.

HELP! I AM A PRISONER IN A TOOTHPASTE FACTORY

JOHN ANTROBUS

The neon sign fixed up by Ronnie's Dad – an electrical genius – in the bathroom said 'NOW CLEAN YOUR TEETH'. When Ronnie does so he gets another message: 'Help! I am a prisoner in a toothpaste factory'.

Ronnie sets off on the toothpaste trail, desperately trying to evade the wicked clutches of the chemist, and when Mum and Dad are imprisoned in Glum's Toothpaste Factory, his mission becomes even more urgent ...

The second in a series of hilarious adventures with fast-paced plots and an eccentric hero.

KNIGHT BOOKS